D0683323

To Nick Maland and the shadows
and Jon Appleton — genius
S.C.

First published in 2013 by Scholastic Children's Books
Euston House, 24 Eversholt Street
London NW1 1DB
a division of Scholastic Ltd
www.scholastic.co.uk
London ~ New York ~ Toronto ~ Sydney ~ Auckland
Mexico City ~ New Delhi ~ Hong Kong

PB ISBN 978 1 407 11727 0

Printed in Singapore

1 3 5 7 9 10 8 6 4 2

Woolly

by Sam Childs

SCHOLASTIC

A long, long time ago, there lived a family of magnificent woolly mammoths – Mummy mammoth, Daddy mammoth and their two mammoth sons, Willy and Wally.

One day, Willy and Wally got a new baby sister.
And because Mummy was woolly and Daddy was woolly
and Willy was woolly and Wally was woolly...

...they called the new
baby WOOLLY.

But there was a problem.

Woolly was not woolly.
Not one bit.

"I'm COLD!" sobbed the new baby.

"You're whaaaat?!" gasped Willy.

"You're pink!" giggled Wally.

"My poor baby!" sighed Mummy.
"Better start knitting," chuckled Daddy.

But Mummy had a better idea.
She wrapped Woolly up
in a tea towel.

Woolly was very excited.
"I'm off to make some
friends!" she cried.

"Hello, I'm Woolly. Would you like to play with me?" she asked a group of friendly looking animals.

But the animals took one look at her and ran as fast as their little legs could carry them, shouting, "It's a sabre-toothed TIGER!"

They left nothing but a cloud of snow behind.

Woolly stomped back home to the cave.
"No one will play with me," she sobbed and tossed away the stripy tea towel.
"I'm COLD!" wept Woolly.
"You're whaaaat?" gasped Willy.
"Still pink!" giggled Wally.

"My poor baby!" sighed Mummy.
"Better start knitting,"
chuckled Daddy.

But Mummy had
a better idea.

The birds helped Mummy gather together some loose feathers and she made Woolly a fluffy new coat.

Woolly was very excited.
"I'm off to make some friends!" she cried.

The other animals all stared in wonder.

"What kind of bird are you?" they asked.

"And can you fly?"

"I can do ANYTHING!" boasted Woolly, and she climbed to the top of a snowy hill, jumped off and FLEW...

...all the way down into a puddle of mud. When she looked up, all the animals had gone.

Woolly marched back to the cave and shook off her feathery coat.
"I'm COLD!" she wailed.
"Whaaaat, cold AGAIN?" gasped Willy.
"And still pink!" giggled Wally.

"My poor baby!" sighed Mummy.
"Better start knitting," chuckled Daddy.

And that's exactly what Mummy did!

Two kind goats gave Mummy
some lovely and soft wool.

Then Mummy knitted and knitted and knitted. And then she knitted some more, until she said, "READY!"

Woolly put on her new suit and cried, "I'm off to make some friends!"

"OOOH!" cried all the animals.
"A baby mammoth with a woolly suit.
Would you like to play with us?"

And Woolly and her new friends
PLAYED and PLAYED and PLAYED.

Every day after that, Woolly put on her woolly suit and went out to play. But on the coldest day of winter, Woolly said...

"I'm HOT!"

"You're NOT!" gasped Willy.

"You're HOT?"
giggled Wally.

Woolly was sooooo hot she raced out of the cave...

...and ran into the cold, cold snow.

As she rushed past a tree, a tiny thread from her suit caught onto a branch...

...and her suit began to unravel.

"My pink woolly baby mammoth!" smiled Mummy.
"Some things are well worth waiting for!" chuckled Daddy.
And they all rushed to give Woolly a MAMMOTH hug!

The End